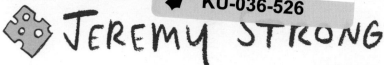

JEREMY STRONG

SMALL TALES FROM THE BIG FOREST

ARMADILLO AND HARE
AND THE
FLAMINGO
AFFAIR

ILLUSTRATED BY REBECCA BAGLEY

David Fickling Books

31 Beaumont Street
Oxford OX1 2NP, UK

Armadillo and Hare and the Flamingo Affair
is a
DAVID FICKLING BOOK

First published in Great Britain in 2021 by
David Fickling Books,
31 Beaumont Street,
Oxford, OX1 2NP

www.davidficklingbooks.com

Hardback edition published 2021
This edition published 2022

Text © Jeremy Strong, 2021
Illustrations © Rebecca Bagley, 2021

978-1-78845-216-8

1 3 5 7 9 10 8 6 4 2

Papers used by David Fickling Books are from
well-managed forests and other responsible sources.

MIX
Paper from
responsible sources
FSC® C018072

DAVID FICKLING BOOKS Reg. No. 8340307

A CIP catalogue record for this book is available from the British Library.

Printed and bound in Great Britain by Clays Ltd, Elcograf S.p.A.

I have dedicated books to my wonderful Gillie before, but as I am now even more dedicated to her I'm making another. Chapter 6 only exists because of Gillie's cucumbers. JS

For Natasha and Nana. Without your help this book would probably not even be halfway done. RB

Contents

A Song Without Words

The night's deep darkness was soft and warm. Hare woke slowly, like a bubble drifting up through water before finally floating on the surface. What was that strange and distant sound? His ears were on alert. If Hare's ears were the hands on a clock they were saying it was ten to two in the morning. Which it was.

Now his ears began to sway gently to the distant song. He got out of bed and padded across to his open window. A light breeze brought the strange and beautiful song closer still.

Hare's bedroom door squeaked open and Armadillo appeared. He was wearing his dressing gown, inside out.

'Ah, you've heard it too,' Armadillo whispered.

'It's wonderful, magical,' Hare murmured. 'But where is it coming from?'

Armadillo grunted. 'No idea. All I can tell is that it's a song without words, but you sort of feel that there are words.'

'And the words are wonderful.' Hare nodded. 'It's so peaceful.'

The two companions stood in the darkness at the window until the song finished. Just as they turned away they heard a distant sing-song whisper on the wind.

'Goodnight, Big Forest. Sweet dreams. Goodnight.'

Armadillo and Hare looked at each other. 'Strange,' muttered Armadillo. 'But beautiful.'

'I've never heard anything like it,' said Hare. 'It was so magical. Ethereal.'

Armadillo's eyes widened and his snout twitched. 'Ethereal, eh? That's a rather splendid word, Hare. Where did it come from?'

'It was in one of my books. I thought I would try and remember it.'

'And so you have. Ethereal. I like that.' Armadillo headed for the door. 'I'm going back to sleep. It's half-past two in the middle of the night.'

Hare smiled to himself in the dark and settled back into bed. He pulled the covers up to his chin. 'Goodnight,' he called out.

But there was only silence and the stars beyond.

Hare was up at daybreak. It was normally Armadillo who put breakfast together because he would be the earliest to get up. Hare liked to spend a bit of time first thing in the morning combing his long ears.

But today felt different. Was it something to do with the singing in the night? Perhaps it was, but Hare felt well rested, happy and – well, bouncy.

Now he bounced around the kitchen, putting out cups and plates, a jar of marmalade, and Armadillo's special tomato jam which he liked to eat with his morning cheese.

'My goodness, you have been busy!' Armadillo stood in the doorway and studied the breakfast table. 'I was just popping down to do all that and now you've done it. Thank you, Hare. What a display! Do you know, I slept like a baby last night.'

'Hmm! Babies don't snore.' Hare smiled. 'And look at you, Armadillo. You've got your dressing gown on inside out, again!'

'I like it like that,' claimed Armadillo. 'It stays cleaner for longer.'

'Not on the inside,' argued Hare.

'But the inside is the outside and the outside is the inside so what you see is the outside, and the outside that was the outside is now the inside. See?'

Hare was creasing up with laughter. 'No,

I don't see. You've exhausted me. A moment ago I was all bouncy. Then you came into the room and I feel as if I've just got a puncture and I'm slowly going down. Like a tyre. Please stop talking in riddles. Come to the table and have some breakfast.'

Armadillo sat down. Soon they were both silent. Hare was munching muesli and Armadillo was chewing cheese.

Then, out of nowhere, the singing began again. They both shot upright and stopped eating. They pushed back their chairs and stared out over the meadow towards the Big Forest. But there was nothing to see. Then they heard a familiar 'ping-ping' and a 'parp-parp' and Wombat came into view on her bicycle. She was doing a handstand on the handlebars. Wombat was good at that sort of thing.

'Isn't it exciting?!' she shouted as she passed the little log cabin. 'Such beee-ooo-tiful singing. All night! It's coming from near the lake! I'm going to see what it is. Come on!'

Hare and Armadillo dropped everything and hurried outside.

As they crossed the dew-spangled meadow they met up with Jaguar and her great friend Invisible Stick Insect.

'Interesting daywear, Armadillo,' Jaguar remarked with a throaty chortle.

Armadillo grunted and snuffled. He tried to think of a smart reply, but couldn't. Anyway, smart replies don't really work if you're wearing your dressing gown inside out.

'It's wonderful singing, isn't it?' squeaked Invisible Stick Insect. She was perched between Jaguar's ears, where she looked like a bit of stick, naturally. 'I wonder who it is.'

When they reached the edge of the lake they realised they were the last to arrive. Lobster, Elephant, Tortoise, Giraffe and Bear (of the polar variety) were already gathered together and staring.

There, right beside the edge of the lake, was a large bath. And in the bath there was an extraordinary bird. She was fabulously pink.

One gorgeous, black-tipped wing was draped over the edge. The long neck and head were decorated with necklaces, a pearl choker, and rainbow-bright feathers like a magnificent crest on her head. She had long eyelashes that fluttered above eyes that sparkled with joy – and mischief.

And, of course, there was the song, which continued, an endless melody that swooped and soared and hovered and dived, only to soar again until it slowly faded away and ceased.

Then the wonderful bird turned her head with its enormous shining beak and gazed back at them. She sat up and opened both wings wide, and everyone gasped. There were feathers upon feathers, ever more colourful, dripping from the tips of her wings.

'Darlings!' she sang. 'Welcome to my world!'

'Her world?' muttered Armadillo. 'It's not her world. It's our world. She's only just arrived!'

'Sssh,' whispered Hare sharply.

'Darlings, sweethearts! I'm so enchanted to see you all. Oh, look at you, Jaguar. Such beauty and grace. And you there, Armadillo. Ha ha! You're outrageous! Wearing your dressing gown! Inside out! I love it. You've made my day, Pops!'

Armadillo's snout almost tied itself into a knot. 'Pops?!' he exploded. 'Since when have I been called Pops?'

He pushed forward, clearing his throat loudly. 'The name,' he said, 'is Armadillo.'

The bird trilled a laugh. 'I know that. But in my heart you will always be Pops, and I love you, darling! You really are quite the thing.'

Armadillo was not at all sure that he wanted to be 'quite the thing'. For a start he wasn't sure what being quite the thing actually meant.

'Look at all of you sweethearts! Aren't you gorgeous?' The bird blew kisses to everyone with her wings. 'I love you all. Let me introduce myself. I am Flamingo, singer, dancer, prancer and performer extraordinaire.' Flamingo rose up and stepped from the bath. The gasp from the crowd was even louder.

Flamingo had legs. She had legs that

seemed to go on, and on – and on.

'Are they telescopic?' asked Tortoise, before toppling backwards from having to stare up so far.

'Phoowee!' said Elephant. 'Sheesh!'

Hare sighed and shook his head. 'Extraordinary,' he murmured. And for once Armadillo was speechless.

Flamingo stepped forward, gave an elegant curtsy and then – shimmered.

With her wings spread, Flamingo made her entire body tremble, so that all the jewels and feathery extensions sparkled and glittered with delight.

Giraffe was entranced. Wombat shook her head as if she couldn't believe such beauty. Hare's ears were dizzy with admiration. Armadillo's eyes simply boggled.

Flamingo soaked up their adoration. 'Darlings, I feel fabulous! I am fabulous!'

Only Lobster crossed her claws over her chest and muttered darkly, 'Who does she think she is? With a bath of all things! Beside a lake? A bath?'

Bear pushed forward and bowed deeply.

'Madam,' he growled. 'I am Bear, of the polar variety, and I am almost a doctor. Furthermore, it may interest you to know that I play the drums.'

Flamingo's eyes widened to huge, glossy, shining discs. 'The drums! But darling, you're a

musician! We must work together! I shall sing like an angel – a large, very pink angel – and you, my sweet, you will hit your . . . things.'

'Drums,' Bear reminded her.

'Yes! We shall make music. We shall dance and sing! Darlings, you are so lucky I am here!'

Several animals in the audience clapped loudly. Tortoise (who had a French mother) even shouted, 'Ooh la la!'

But Armadillo nudged his friend hard and hissed in his ear, 'She called me Pops!'

The Mystery of the Bath

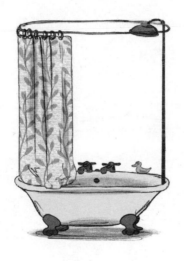

reakfast was being unusually noisy. Armadillo banged the coffee pot down on the table. 'Pops!' he exploded. He let two mugs come crashing down. 'Pops! Pops!'

Hare watched from the doorway. One ear was up and one was down. 'I think "Pops" is rather cute,' he said.

'Cute?' Armadillo exploded again.

'Yes. Flamingo obviously likes you,' Hare suggested mischievously. 'Not to mention your inside-out dressing gown.'

'Well, I certainly don't like . . . ' Armadillo

broke off suddenly. He shook his head in confusion and growled, mostly at himself. He did like Flamingo. A lot.

Flamingo was exciting. Flamingo sang like an angel. Flamingo was flamboyant, thrilling and utterly . . . coral. Yes, coral was a better word than pink. Coral was a special, deep kind of pink and Flamingo was certainly special.

Armadillo poured coffee into the mugs. He grumbled on. 'Of course I like Flamingo. But I don't like being called "Pops". It makes me feel old.'

Hare reached across the table and patted Armadillo's paw. 'My friend, you are old.'

'I know, but I don't like feeling it.'

'Why don't you tell Flamingo that you don't want to be called "Pops"?'

'I thought of that, but she will probably call me "darling" instead and that's even worse.'

Hare laughed. 'She calls everyone "darling". You must have noticed. I think that maybe she's come from a theatre.'

Armadillo's eyes twinkled. 'An escaped actress,' he suggested. 'Imagine that. It would be a bit like having an escaped prisoner here. How exciting!'

Hare didn't think Flamingo had escaped from anything. He sat back in his chair and slowly sipped his coffee. The two of them were soon lost in exotic and wildly pink thoughts.

Or coral, in Armadillo's case.

The two friends were interrupted by a loud 'ping-ping' from outside, quickly followed by a 'parp-parp'.

'That will be Wombat,' Armadillo declared. 'I had better put that cheese back in the fridge before she sees it.'

Hare looked at Armadillo over his glasses. 'I don't think Wombat eats cheese.'

'Good. But I'm not going to risk it,' said Armadillo as there was a knock at the door. 'You answer that.'

It wasn't just Wombat who had come to visit. Lobster was with her. Lobster liked to ride in the basket on the front of Wombat's bicycle.

'Hello!' said Wombat, cheerfully sniffing

the air. 'Ah – coffee.
Is there any left?'

'You are
w e l c o m e
to coffee,'
Armadillo
said, rather
grandly. 'But I'm
afraid we have no cheese.'

Lobster waved a large claw as if she wasn't
bothered with coffee or cheese. She didn't
look happy. Nobody was quite sure just what
Lobster would look like if she was happy. For
some reason she was nearly always disgruntled,
annoyed or upset. Occasionally she was all
three at once. Maybe it came from being
underwater most of the time.

Hare thought that if he spent most of his time underwater he'd probably get a bit fed up.

Now Lobster folded her claws across her chest and eyed all three of them, one after the other. 'Well?' she snapped. 'What are we going to do?'

Armadillo and Hare looked at each other and shrugged. Do about what?

Wombat explained. 'Lobster is concerned about Flamingo. She came to tell me all about it.' She glanced at Hare and Armadillo. Maybe she winked. Wombat put a paw to her eye as if there was something in it. 'I said we should talk to Armadillo and Hare because they are good listeners. Armadillo is very old—'

'Oh dear,' muttered Armadillo.

'And sensible,' Wombat added quickly, 'and Hare is a good listener because he has such long ears.'

Hare gave a proud smile and pulled at each of his fabulously long ears in turn.

Lobster, however, was not interested in anyone's ears. She pushed herself forward. 'We are talking about Flamingo,' she said crisply.

Armadillo raised his eyebrows. 'Are we?'

'Yes. What's she doing here? And why on earth is she sitting in a bath right beside the lake? Isn't there enough water in the lake? How did she get a bath here? Where on earth has she come from?'

Armadillo smiled. 'Hare thinks she's an escaped prisoner,' he drawled teasingly.

'No I didn't,' protested Hare. 'That was

you. I said a theatre, not a prison.'

But it was too late. Lobster seized on the new information and held it with both claws. 'An escaped prisoner! I might have known. Of course, it all makes sense now. The bath, everything.'

Armadillo shook his old, grey head. 'Well, I'm glad it makes sense for you, Lobster, but I don't understand why Flamingo has a bath.'

'Because she stole it, of course. That's why she was in prison.'

Wombat frowned. 'But if Flamingo was in prison for stealing a bath, she wouldn't have it after she escaped, would she?'

Lobster rolled her little black eyes. 'Flamingo escaped and collected the bath from where she had hidden it before she went to prison,' she explained. 'Or she escaped and immediately stole another bath. I bet that's what she did. Once you start stealing baths you can't stop. She's probably got lots of them.'

Armadillo held up two paws. 'Everyone, please stop talking nonsense. Now listen to me, especially you, Lobster. None of us know where Flamingo has come from. She is not an escaped prisoner. She has not been stealing baths. None of us even know Flamingo. She only arrived a day or so ago. We can't go around judging someone when we don't know anything about them.'

'She's different,' snapped Lobster.

Armadillo snorted with laughter. 'Lobster! Look at us. Giraffe, with his extraordinary long neck, Invisible Stick Insect, Bear, with his drums, you, me – we're all different.'

Armadillo chuckled again and nodded. 'We must give Flamingo time. We must get to know her. After all, she is a wonderful singer.'

'Pffff!' hissed Lobster. 'I can sing better than she can, but only underwater.'

'I think Armadillo is right,' said Wombat. 'You see, Lobster? I knew it would be a good idea to ask an old and wise person. I think having Flamingo around could be fun.'

'Well said,' agreed Hare, polishing his glasses with the end of his scarf.

All three of them turned to Lobster.

She eyed them beadily. 'We shall see. All right, we will give Flamingo a chance. However, I am quite sure that you will all regret your decision. And

don't blame me if your bath suddenly vanishes. Then you'll be sorry!'

Lobster marched out to Wombat's bicycle and hauled herself into the basket. Wombat glanced at Armadillo and Hare. She shrugged and set off with Lobster.

Armadillo and Hare stood at the door and watched them leave. Armadillo took a deep breath, let out a long sigh and relaxed.

'I do like it when life is interesting and full of questions,' he said. 'And the funny thing is it always makes me think that cheese is the answer. If you'll excuse me, Hare, I think I might go and visit the fridge.'

Too Much Exercising

Hare was doing his morning exercises. Staying in good shape was important for Hare. Looking good was also important, and Hare was wearing his new gym kit. His dark-blue shorts had a lime-green lightning flash on each side. His red top had an even larger matching lime-green flash on the chest.

'Very smart,' Armadillo said in a dry voice. 'Does it help you run faster?'

'Don't be annoying,' said Hare. 'You should exercise too. It keeps you healthy.'

'So you keep telling me.' Armadillo shook

his head. 'It quite wears me out just watching you. If I had to do them as well as watch you I'd be flat on my back and panting in no time at all.'

Hare laughed. 'Well, I have some new breathing exercises that are really good for you – and easy too.'

Armadillo's head lifted sharply. 'Breathing? Hare, I breathe all day. Look – in, out, in out. If I wasn't breathing I'd be dead.'

Hare could hardly speak. 'Stop it, Armadillo. I can't do the exercises if I'm laughing. This is good for your lungs. You hold your breath for a minute. Come on, I bet you can't do it.'

Armadillo shuffled back into his armchair. 'Of course I can. Go on. I'm ready.'

Hare settled down. 'Take a deep breath, slowly breathe in and hold it – now.'

They both held their breath. After a few seconds Armadillo's whiskers started to fidget. After a few more seconds his snout turned purple, then blue. He opened his mouth a fraction on one side and took a sneaky new breath.

Hare didn't notice. His eyes were closed and his ears had drooped down over his shoulders. He was so still that Armadillo began to wonder if his friend was still alive. 'Hare? Hare?'

There was no answer. Armadillo was worried. He went across to his friend and poked him.

Hare opened one eye. 'You're hopeless, Armadillo. You're supposed to be holding your

breath.'

'I did, for about a week. I was worried about you. I thought you'd died.'

Hare frowned and shook his head. 'It's an exercise. I know you think it's all a waste of time, but it's good for you and I want you to stay healthy.'

Armadillo patted Hare's shoulder. 'You're so

thoughtful, Hare, but I don't think armadillos are built for exercise. It's not an armadillo kind of thing. You do your workouts. I have got a little project of my own in mind.'

'Really?' Hare's ears perked up.

'Yes. I have decided to grow some vegetables. I was rather hoping I might be able to grow cheese too, but sadly you can't. However, I can make a vegetable garden. You carry on breathing, Hare, there's a good chap. I've got some digging to do.'

Later on that morning, Hare cleared away the breakfast things. From time to time he glanced out of the kitchen window. Armadillo was digging.

Armadillo dug the ground for at least

an hour. Every so often he would stop for a moment to rest and catch his breath. Eventually he had a good-sized rectangle of earth ready for planting.

Inside the kitchen, Hare watched Armadillo and smiled. What a lot of exercise his friend was getting!

At last Armadillo put aside his spade and

came back to the house. He pulled up one end of his cardigan and wiped the sweat and mud from his beaming face.

'There! Have you seen my vegetable patch?'

'Well done!' said Hare. He wanted to point out to Armadillo how much exercise he had done while digging, but he knew it would have simply made Armadillo rather cross. Instead he asked Armadillo what he was planning to grow.

'Ah!' Armadillo's eyes twinkled. 'I've been thinking about that. Lettuce and carrots! I know those are two of your favourites. Tomatoes, beans, onions, herbs and anything else I think of.'

'Perfect,' said Hare. 'Let's sit on the porch. You look as if you need a cool drink.'

'And a cheese sandwich,' Armadillo added.

'With tomato jam.'

So they took glasses, a big jug of water and a cheese sandwich from the fridge and went out to the front porch. There they sat gazing across the peaceful meadow to the Big Forest which seemed to be dozing under the morning sun.

Armadillo sank happily back into his armchair. 'This is the life,' he murmured.

'Lettuce and carrots,' Hare repeated dreamily. 'That is definitely the life.'

At that moment there was a loud crashing noise from the edge of the Big Forest. The trees and bushes shook crazily. Suddenly a large, hulking brown shape burst out of the trees. It stood for a moment, then set off at high speed, thundering across the meadow. The ground shook and the porch of the log cabin trembled.

Armadillo sighed. 'Oh dear. Angry Bison is back.'

Hare frowned. 'Angry Bison?'

Armadillo nodded. His snout wrinkled. 'He turns up every now and then. We haven't seen him for ages. He never stays long, just comes

and goes. Try and keep out of his way, Hare.'

Hare's ears twitched nervously. 'Is he dangerous?'

Armadillo considered this. 'It's best to avoid him if possible. He's rather big and he likes to charge straight at you. Look, look! There's Wombat on her bike. She hasn't seen him, but he's seen her!'

'Will Wombat be all right?' asked Hare, his ears twisting into knots.

'Hmmm. Probably.'

Hare's eyes grew round. Probably? That was not very reassuring.

Angry Bison charged at full speed towards Wombat. She had stopped in the middle of the meadow. Bison thundered to a halt in a cloud of dust right in front of her.

Armadillo and Hare could clearly hear him bellowing at her, 'Get out of my way!'

They saw Wombat carefully move her bike to one side. Angry Bison snorted and went thundering on, back to the forest. Wombat got back on her bike. She spotted Armadillo and Hare on the porch and waved at them cheerfully. Then she went on her way.

'There,' said Armadillo. 'Now you know what Angry Bison does. After a few days he'll go away and huff and puff somewhere else. He always does.'

'But he had the whole meadow to run around in,' Hare complained.

'Exactly.'

Hare folded his arms crossly. 'That's stupid.'

'It's what he does, stupid or not, and I'm not going

to pick an argument with an angry bison.' Armadillo examined the crumbs on his plate. 'I think I might have another one of those,' he murmured.

But Hare was upset. There was the meadow, blossoming with flowers and humming with soft bees. There was the quiet blue sky and warm sunshine. It was all so peaceful. How could anyone be so angry, and rude? Hare's ears scratched each other. It was all rather strange and bothersome.

'Cucumbers,' Armadillo said, out of the blue.

'Sorry?' Hare was quickly brought out of his thoughts.

'Cucumbers,' Armadillo repeated. 'In the vegetable patch. What do you think?'

'Yes, definitely.' Hare got to his feet. 'I'm going to do my afternoon exercises now.'

'Oh goodness!' said Armadillo. 'Just watching Angry Bison dashing about has worn me out. I'm going to have a snooze.'

Hare smiled to himself. He knew exactly why Armadillo was so tired, and it had nothing to do with bisons.

A Wardrobe and a
Lamp Post?

Flamingo had sung her dream-song all through the night. Her lullaby had caressed every creature, and every leaf and blade of grass of the Big Forest. The stars had glittered in their billions until dawn arrived. Now the forest shimmered in the heat of the early morning. Elephant was going through his morning routine.

1. Stretch trunk.

2. Roll in the mud.

3. Noisily blow bubbles

4. Wash mud off and get dry.

5. Skipping (fifty times).

Elephant found skipping the most difficult. After all, he was an elephant and skipping does not come naturally to pachyderms. One end of a long rope was tied to a tree. The other was tied to his tail. Swishing his tail whilst jumping at the same time was not easy. The most skips Elephant had ever managed was three. However, the most important part of the exercise was not to give up.

But today Elephant was faced with a problem. He had a favourite tree that he liked to tie his rope to. But this morning there was a wardrobe standing in the way.

Elephant stared at it. He looked at it from the right and then from the left. He even looked behind it.

Nothing changed Elephant's opinion that

this was indeed a wardrobe. And it was in front of his favourite tree. What was he to do?

'That's a big wardrobe,' said Jaguar, slipping silently out of the nearby bushes.

'Phoowee! Jaguar! You made me jump.'

'I noticed,' said Jaguar, cleaning her whiskers. 'Is it yours?'

Elephant shook his head. 'I have no idea whose it is or how it got here.'

A tiny voice spoke up. 'Look inside!' It was Invisible Stick Insect.

'Oh, hello, Stick Insect,' said Elephant. 'I thought you were there somewhere.'

'I'm waving. Over here.'

Elephant didn't bother to look too hard. When you looked for Invisible Stick Insect you only ever saw a bunch of twigs. 'Oh yes, there you are,' he said, not wanting to hurt Stick Insect's feelings.

Elephant knew that even the smallest things have feelings. And even though they might be small feelings, if you are actually small those small feelings are pretty big.

The three of them looked at the wardrobe and the wardrobe silently gazed back at them. It was so big. What might be hiding inside?

'I think we'd better tell the others,' suggested Elephant, and so they set off for the meadow and Armadillo's log cabin. On the way they met Giraffe, Lobster and Wombat.

Having heard Elephant's story, Armadillo and Hare wanted to see the mysterious wardrobe themselves. When they reached the wardrobe they found Bear (of the polar variety) and Tortoise, both staring at it.

'This is very strange,' remarked Bear.

'Hmm. Is there a lamp post nearby?' Tortoise wondered.

The others looked at him quizzically.

'Tortoise, why might there be a lamp post?' asked Jaguar.

Tortoise smiled nervously. 'It was just an idea of mine.'

'I think we should look inside,' said Armadillo. Several of the others moved back, even Elephant, until his rear came up against a tree.

Armadillo turned the handle of the wardrobe. 'It's locked,' he said, and the animals shuffled forward again. 'If we had a twig we could try and pick the lock.'

'I'm a bit like a twig,' said Invisible Stick Insect. 'Maybe I could climb inside the lock and open it.'

'Sheesh! That is very brave of you,' said Elephant admiringly.

So Invisible Stick Insect climbed inside the lock. She soon found out how to make the catch spring back. The door of the wardrobe swung open.

'Phoowee!' whistled Elephant.

'Well I never,' murmured Tortoise.

'Extraordinary,' said Hare.

'I say,' muttered Giraffe, from on high.

Armadillo nodded. 'It's quite a collection.'

The wardrobe was full of clothes, feathers, boxes of make-up and jewellery galore. There were necklaces by the dozen, bracelets and bangles, tiaras, crowns, finger- toe- ear- and nose-rings – all glittering in the sunlight.

And the clothes were not ordinary. There were exotic cloaks, strange eye masks, wonderfully coloured shoes, jackets with hundreds of little jewels sewn onto them and boots – boots that would only fit someone with very long, thin legs.

As the animals stared at the contents of the

wardrobe they heard a fluttering from above. They looked up and saw a pink angel slowly descending between the trees. The angel had a large beak and very long, thin legs.

'Darlings!' Flamingo cried with delight. 'You've found my wardrobe! I knew it was around here somewhere. Isn't it wonderful? Oh, I'm so happy to be reunited. Here are all the costumes for my brilliant shows.'

Flamingo pulled out a long feathered boa and flung it round her neck. She swept up several necklaces and bracelets, handing them to her audience and blowing a kiss at Armadillo.

'Pops! Your cardigan! Buttons undone all over the place. You're such a rebel! I love it! Have a brooch or three! And Giraffe, oh my goodness, those necklaces go so well with your spots.'

Lobster eyed Flamingo suspiciously. She tapped the tall bird's ankle, which was about as high as she could reach. 'How did you get this wardrobe here?' she grumbled. 'First of all you produce a bath out of nowhere, and now a wardrobe – full of jewellery! Is it stolen? How do we know it's yours?'

Flamingo bent down and spoke in a low voice. 'Lobster, sweetheart, a lady never tells her secrets.'

Lobster was unimpressed. 'Well, I'm a lady too, and I don't think ladies should have secrets. I certainly don't.'

Flamingo gasped with horror. 'But darling, you poor thing! You can have some of mine! Lean closer so I can whisper in your ear.'

Lobster, fascinated, leaned in and listened. Her eyes almost popped out and she turned bright red. 'No! I don't believe it!'

Flamingo nodded slowly and silently. Lobster blushed ever more deeply. She didn't ask any further questions.

'Now then, darling Elephant,' said Flamingo. 'You look like a sturdy chap. Lovely, lovely legs. So shapely! Like a grand piano I once knew. Do you think you might help get my wardrobe down to the lake, sweetie?'

Elephant stepped forward proudly. 'I shall be honoured to help,' he announced.

'I can help too,' droned Giraffe. 'I'm – quite strong in the muscle department.'

'Me too,' said Hare, whiskers and ears twitching at the thought of helping such a fantastically pink and glamorous creature.

'Don't be silly, Hare,' said Armadillo. 'Wardrobes are beyond you.'

'Darling, gallant Hare, a little bird told me you play a magical tuba. How perfectly wonderful. Why don't you get your tuba and play us a marching tune,' cried Flamingo. 'Then we shall be at the lake in no time at all.'

Hare fetched his tuba. Soon everyone was stomping along, with the wardrobe tied to

Elephant's back.

Flamingo sang to Hare's marching tune, and out of the tuba floated a military band, magicians' hats, tiny white rabbits, three toilet rolls, several coat hangers and five pairs of long

evening gloves with fake-fur cuffs.

The wardrobe was placed near the bath.

'Darlings, thank you, thank you. And now I am so happy I shall give you a little show.'

Flamingo gave a deep curtsy, disappeared inside her wardrobe and pulled the door shut.

For a few moments there was silence.

Then the wardrobe began to sing. Of course the animals knew it was Flamingo inside – but suddenly something extraordinary happened.

Flamingo's head appeared out of the top of the wardrobe. Her beak was pointed at the sky and both her eyes and beak were closed. But the wardrobe was still singing!

Flamingo rose higher and higher. As her wings cleared the wardrobe sides they spread wide, showing all the glittering feather extensions.

And still she rose into the air, wings slowly beating, with the song ringing from the wardrobe. The audience burst into wild applause.

'How does she do that?' Hare whispered to

his companion.

Armadillo was in raptures. 'Ventriloquism. She's a ventriloquist. She's a singer, an acrobat, a performer and she's absolutely divine!'

Hare looked at his friend. One long ear was astonished. The other was surprised. As for his whiskers, they were flabbergasted.

An Invitation

Armadillo was on the porch. He was listening to Flamingo's soft singing weave its way amongst the swaying trees of the Big Forest. He was still in his dressing gown. Somehow, this morning, he had managed to wear it the right way round.

Now he stood with his hands in his pockets, swaying a little like the trees of the Big Forest. And at that moment an idea popped into his head.

Armadillo smiled to himself. It was a good idea. He went into the cabin, found some paper and a pen and began to write. As he concentrated, his snout wiggled and his tongue stuck out at one side.

He began:

Dear Flamingo, I hope you are well. I am well.

That was how Hare found his friend, crouching over the paper. 'Ah,' said Hare. 'I was just thinking of doing something like that myself. Where did you find the paper?'

Armadillo grunted. He didn't want to be disturbed. 'There's more paper around somewhere,' he told Hare. 'What do you want it for?'

'Oh, just an idea,' murmured Hare. 'What are you doing?'

Armadillo sighed. He put down his pen. 'If you must know, Hare, I am writing to Flamingo. I am inviting her for dinner this evening.'

Hare's eyes turned into saucers. His ears did a rapid whirligig movement which left them twisted into the most complicated knot.

'But, but, but that is exactly what I was planning to do!' he cried, waving the paper he had just found, and a second pen.

'And I've already started,' Armadillo pointed out.

Hare was speechless. He collapsed back into a chair and his ears collapsed with him.

Armadillo stopped writing. He looked at his beginning. *Dear Flamingo, I hope you are well. I am well.* It didn't sound very interesting. He glanced across at his friend, slumped in the armchair. He couldn't invite Flamingo to the log cabin and leave Hare just hanging around, twiddling his ears. Armadillo sighed.

'Why don't we both ask Flamingo to dinner?' Armadillo suggested. 'You can play your tuba and I can tell her the history of cheese since dinosaur times.'

Hare sat up. His ears sat up. Even his whiskers sat up. He wasn't sure if dinosaurs had dined on cheese but he was grateful to hear Armadillo's offer.

'Thank you.'

Armadillo grunted again. 'Now then, listen. I have got as far as Dear Flamingo, I hope you are well. What do you think?'

'It's a bit – dull?' suggested Hare.

'It is. It makes me want to crawl back to bed just reading it.'

Hare scratched one ear with the other. 'Why don't we make it a proper invitation, with big letters in different colours. You know, something like . . . We cordially invite you to dine with Armadillo

and Hare on Monday evening at their lovely home in the meadow.'

'I like the sound of that,' Armadillo nodded. 'Very grand. Dinner is the most important meal of the day. Flamingo will be impressed. Let's get to work. I'll draw the letters. You colour them in.'

And that is what they did. It took a while. That was because Armadillo wrote his own name with only one 'L'. Then Hare managed to knock over the jar of red paint with one of his phenomenally long ears. It slopped across the invitation.

'Shall we start again?' Armadillo suggested.

So they did.

It was almost lunch time before they had the invitation ready. Hare rolled it up and Armadillo tied a pink ribbon round it.

'Flamingo likes pink,' he told Hare, and they set off across the meadow towards the lake. Hare kept glancing around in case Angry Bison suddenly decided to put in an appearance, but he didn't.

When the two friends arrived at the lake they found Flamingo in her bath. She peered at them over the top of one lifted wing.

'Darlings! You've caught me in my bath!

I was just washing my hair. I must look an absolute nightmare!'

Armadillo turned his back and faced the other way before spluttering apologies.

Hare simply stared. He had never seen anything quite so wet and bedraggled.

'You just wait there, darlings, while I fluff myself up a bit. There. I feel much better now. Pops, sweetie, do turn round.'

Flamingo stepped from the bath on her extraordinarily long legs. She lowered her equally long neck until her head was on the same level as Armadillo and Hare. She fluttered her eyelashes at them both.

'Good morning, sweethearts! I am all yours. Now then, to what do I owe this pleasure?'

Armadillo coughed and cleared his throat. 'It's like this. Hare and I have been thinking and we would like to—' Armadillo broke off. He thrust the rolled-up invitation towards

Flamingo. 'It's all in there,' he said, blushing.

'Oh, darlings! This is heavenly! All rolled up and tied with some fabulous pink ribbon. It looks very grand. Am I being given an award?'

Hare stepped forward. 'It's an invitation. You'll see.'

Flamingo unrolled the invitation and read it through. 'Oh!' she cried. 'Um, well, um—'

'Would you like to come for dinner tonight?' Armadillo asked.

'Oh dear. Oh dear. Well, the thing is, darlings, Bear (of the something variety) has already asked me to dinner tonight.'

'Has he?' growled Armadillo.

'So perhaps you could come tomorrow night, Tuesday?' suggested Hare brightly.

'I would love to . . .' Flamingo began.

'Normally. But Tuesday, you see, Giraffe has asked for Tuesday.' She looked at Armadillo and Hare with her bright, bright eyes.

Armadillo took a deep breath. 'Wednesday?'

'Elephant,' Flamingo said quickly.

'Thursday?'

'Tortoise.'

' T o r — ! ' Armadillo almost exploded. 'What about Friday?'

'Invisible Stick Insect. We're going to discuss hairstyles. She has so many ideas in that clever little head of hers.'

A long silence followed. Beyond Flamingo, the lake quietly glistened. There was no wind to ruffle its calm surface.

'We'd better get back home,' Armadillo announced, turning to Hare.

'Oh. Yes. Home,' Hare answered. They turned and began to head back the way they had come.

The pair had almost disappeared amongst the trees when Flamingo called after them, 'Darlings! Just a moment, please. I don't suppose – have you had breakfast? Would you like to take breakfast with me? Now?'

'It's lunch time,' Armadillo pointed out.

The Big Forest echoed with Flamingo's laughter. 'Oh, Pops! You're such a hoot. Breakfast, lunch, dinner – it's all food, no matter what time you eat it. Let's be daring, darlings, and have breakfast at lunch time!

What a thrill!'

Flamingo opened her welcoming wings wide and looked at them rather coyly. She closed both eyes slowly, and when she opened them once more they seemed brighter and more charming than ever.

'Darlings! Please take breakfast with me –
at lunch time.'

So they did.

And it was so enjoyable Armadillo quite
forgot to give Flamingo his history of cheese
since dinosaur times.

On their way home Armadillo pointed out that they had managed to share a meal with Flamingo before Bear (of the polar variety).

'Or any of the others,' added Hare.

Armadillo humphed with satisfaction. 'Breakfast is much more important than dinner, Hare. People are always inviting each other to dinner, but having breakfast with someone is Very Special Indeed.'

'Even when you have it at lunch time?' Hare asked.

'Especially when you have it at lunch time.' Armadillo nodded seriously. 'You see, Hare, the world is made up of those who do the same and those who do differently. And I think the ones who do differently are the interesting ones. They are the ones who will change the world.'

Hare agreed. 'You certainly do things differently. But I don't think putting buttons in the wrong holes on your cardigan is going to change the world much at all.'

Armadillo gave Hare a sharp look. 'Sometimes I wonder why I like you.'

Too Many Cucumbers

Rain dripped from the leaves of all the trees in the Big Forest. It refreshed the meadow and watered Armadillo's vegetable plot. His plants were doing well. Armadillo looked at them with satisfaction. In the distance he noticed Angry Bison thundering round the far meadow before crashing back into the trees. It was a normal day in the Big Forest.

Armadillo returned to his vegetables. The tomatoes were ripening fast. His onions were sprouting. The beans were long and fat and hanging from their bean poles.

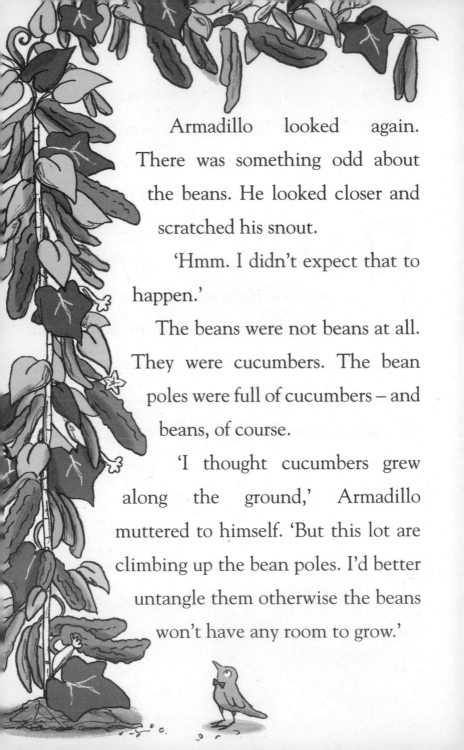

Armadillo looked again. There was something odd about the beans. He looked closer and scratched his snout.

'Hmm. I didn't expect that to happen.'

The beans were not beans at all. They were cucumbers. The bean poles were full of cucumbers – and beans, of course.

'I thought cucumbers grew along the ground,' Armadillo muttered to himself. 'But this lot are climbing up the bean poles. I'd better untangle them otherwise the beans won't have any room to grow.'

He began to pick the ripe cucumbers and untangle their stalks. He pushed amongst the bean sticks as he tried to separate the cucumber plants from the bean plants. It was fiddly, hot work.

All at once there was a small cry from somewhere near Armadillo's knees.

'Help! Help!'

Armadillo knew that his knees weren't calling for help, so where was the cry coming from? Then he spotted Mouse clinging to his cardigan.

'My home! My pocket home! It's disappearing!' Mouse cried.

That was when Armadillo realised the full horror of the

situation. It was not just Mouse's home that was vanishing. It was his favourite cardigan! While he had been picking cucumbers, the bottom of his cardigan had got snagged on a bean pole. Now the cardigan was unravelling at speed. It had already taken off the bottom of the pocket where Mouse often slept.

'Oh! Oh!' Armadillo panicked. He scooped up Mouse and then simply stood, not knowing what to do next. Should he go back and try and rescue the long thread of wool from all the poles and plants that he had been amongst? He couldn't go forward because then his cardigan would unravel even more.

'Mouse, we're trapped!' Armadillo wailed. He lifted his head and shouted, 'Hare! Hare!'

Moments later Hare came rushing from the

house. He was waving a large saucepan. Maybe he had been expecting to find a burglar. He certainly did not expect to find a very sorrowful Armadillo. His friend was standing amongst the bean plants, wet from all the leaves after the rain. He was holding an equally wet Mouse in one paw and a large cucumber in the other, and wearing half a cardigan.

Armadillo gazed at his friend, his eyes overcome with sadness. He didn't speak. A picture tells a thousand words, and

Hare saw it all in seconds.

'Oh my dear, dear friend,' he said. Hare's ears were hugging each other. 'Stand still. I shall get some scissors.'

'You can't cut the thread!' Armadillo exclaimed.

Hare took a deep breath. 'It's the only way,' he said.

Armadillo's eyes glistened and he lowered his head in silence. Hare raced back to the kitchen. When he returned he had the scissors. He traced the thread of caught wool as far back as he could and then – snip. It was done.

The three of them trudged back to the house through the mud. It felt like a funeral procession, with a lifeless cardigan. Armadillo's favourite.

Armadillo took himself upstairs to his bedroom. He lay down on his bed. He was so upset he couldn't even face a big cheese sandwich. Instead he tried to shut out the disaster by closing his eyes and falling asleep.

Downstairs Hare was thinking hard. How could he rescue the situation? How on earth could he bring back a favourite cardigan that had been destroyed!

Hare got out his tuba and began to play. Sometimes playing his tuba helped Hare sort out his thoughts. Soon the room began to fill with all the things that floated out of the tuba and slowly melted away.

101

There were socks – but none that matched. There were balls of wool in different colours, knitting needles, several rocking chairs, three small sheep, a toilet roll (of course), and a tiny wombat.

Hare stared at the miniature wombat as it faded away. His ears suddenly stood up straight and alert. Yes. He knew what to do. He threw a scarf round his neck. It was a new, deep-green scarf which Hare felt matched his rather snazzy deep-green shoes. And so he set off.

It did not take long to reach Wombat's burrow and Wombat was pleased to see him.

'Hare! I was just making a cup of tea. Would you like some? I have some lemon drizzle cake too.'

Hare sat down in a comfortable armchair.

He relayed the whole sad story of the cardigan to Wombat.

'Of course I can help,' said Wombat. 'I know Armadillo's old cardigan was blue, and sadly I don't have any wool that colour. But I do have a rather nice deep-red wool which will match his favourite red slippers.'

Hare smiled. 'Perfect,' he said, stretching out his legs so that Wombat could admire his shoes. 'Having clothes that match is essential. If my clothes don't match it makes me feel jumpy all day.'

'Just one problem,' Wombat went on, ignoring Hare's shoes. 'I'm no good at knitting pockets. I'm brilliant at sleeves, but pockets are beyond me.'

Hare considered this. 'Hmm. I know someone who might be able to help out there.'

The two friends drank their tea and Hare had three slices of lemon drizzle cake before he headed back to the log cabin. Every time he crossed the meadow now he watched out for Angry Bison. It was all getting rather annoying.

The next few days were difficult for Armadillo and Hare. The house was filled with the misery of the lost cardigan. Armadillo went about in his dressing gown. Sometimes it was the right way out. Sometimes it wasn't. Either way, it was not his beloved cardigan. Meanwhile Hare could not tell Armadillo about his secret plan. Suppose it didn't work?

Armadillo spent most of his time wandering around with a wheelbarrow full of spare cucumbers.

'Would anyone like some cucumbers?' he asked whenever he saw a friend.

Elephant did. 'They're good for the bags under my eyes,' he told Armadillo.

'You're welcome.'

'I'll have some,' declared Tortoise. 'I like cold cucumber soup in the hot weather.'

'You're welcome.'

Jaguar was less impressed. 'It's a vegetable. No thank you.'

'You're welcome.'

Hare began to think that if this went on much longer Armadillo would turn into a speaking robot.

And then, at last, there was a knock at the door. It was Wombat. In her arms she had a parcel. It was wrapped in brown paper and tied with a length of deep-red wool.

'It's for you,' Hare told Armadillo.

'Really?' Armadillo was not interested.

'Open it,' Hare suggested.

Armadillo sighed. He heaved himself over to the parcel, as if it was the last thing he wanted to do before dying.

Hare was cross. 'Stop it. Stop feeling sorry for yourself. Just open it.'

Armadillo looked at his companion in surprise, but he opened the parcel. He pulled out the cardigan. He stared at it and felt its softness. He held it against his red slippers. He

examined it and his eyebrows went up a bit.
'It's got a Mouse pocket,' he announced.

Mouse herself poked out her head. 'I knitted
it myself,' she laughed.

Armadillo's eyebrows went up even more.
'It's got three sleeves!'

'Ah!' said Wombat cheerfully. 'I like doing
sleeves and I realised I'd done one too many.
Then I thought maybe it will come in useful
sometime?'

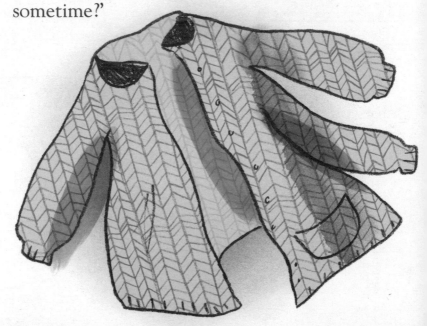

Armadillo could not stop laughing. Eventually he managed to splutter, 'I can always keep spare cucumbers in it.' He turned to his friends with a big smile on his face. 'It's perfect,' he told them. 'Absolutely perfect. Look how it matches my slippers.'

Wombat grinned. 'I put in an extra buttonhole too because I know what you're like. I also put in an extra button – because I really do know what you're like!'

Armadillo slipped on the cardigan. 'Do you know,' he began proudly, 'I think I'm probably the only armadillo in the whole world who has a cardigan with three sleeves.'

And, of course, Armadillo was right.

Armadillo's Special Soup

The Big Forest was unusually quiet. For two days and two nights there had been no singing. Flamingo was silent. Slowly the news spread amongst the animals.

Bear told Tortoise. Tortoise told Giraffe. Giraffe told Lobster and Lobster told everyone else.

'Flamingo can't sing,' Hare repeated to Armadillo. 'She has a sore throat.'

'Oh dear. That's a lot of soreness. Flamingo's throat is so long.'

They were both concerned about Flamingo

and tried to think of something they could do to help.

Hare played his tuba while he thought. It was the sort of soothing melody you might play to someone who was ill. A few bandages floated out of the top of his tuba. These were followed by several bottles of medicine, a hot-water-bottle, a small hospital bed and an ambulance.

Meanwhile Armadillo sat in a chair and thought about what he might do to help. He watched the ambulance slowly fade away. All at once he sat up straight.

'I've got the answer!'

Hare sighed. 'You think it's a cheese sandwich, don't you?'

'Not at all, Hare, no – it's something even

better. What Flamingo needs is some of my Special Soup.'

A loud snort burst from Hare's tuba and a large, warty, green monster climbed out of the instrument. It flicked its fat spongy tongue at

them both, before slowly fading away.

Hare laid the tuba to one side and looked at Armadillo in horror. 'Not your ghastly green soup?'

Armadillo's eyes narrowed. 'Yes, Hare. My ghastly green soup, as you like to call it. You may remember that you got better very quickly that time you were ill.'

'Only because I couldn't bear to drink any more of it!'

Armadillo smiled. 'So the soup worked. You got better.'

'But—' began Hare.

'No buts. I am going to make Flamingo my Special Soup.' And Armadillo stomped off to the kitchen.

Hare's head was spinning. His ears were

spinning. That ghastly green soup tasted awful. Flamingo should be warned. What could he do? The soup would take at least an hour. That gave plenty of time for Hare to hurry over to Flamingo.

Hare grabbed a jacket and scarf, reached the front door and stopped. This was awful. Was he betraying his friend? He took a step forward. He took a step back. His ears pointed in every direction. Finally they both shot forward and Hare followed, hurrying across the meadow.

He was halfway there before he saw Angry Bison ahead of him, right in his path. Hare stopped immediately. Everyone knew Bison was dangerous. Nobody knew what he would do next. And he had horns.

Just for once Angry Bison was standing still. He was quietly munching the grasses and flowers of the meadow.

Hare had never understood why Bison had to charge around telling everyone they were in his way. Nobody liked to be spoken to in that gruff manner. Maybe Bison didn't realise?

It seemed to Hare that today was a day for telling people what he really thought. He was going to tell Flamingo about the ghastly green soup, and now he was going to tell Angry Bison something too. Yes. He had made up his mind.

Hare hurried across the meadow, aiming straight for Angry Bison. He soon reached the creature. Oh my! Up close, Bison was gigantic.

Luckily Hare's brave mood was gigantic too.

'You're in my way!' Hare shouted. 'Move!'

Angry Bison stopped chewing. He raised his head a little and looked at Hare.

'Go on, move!' Hare repeated. 'Get out of my way!'

Angry Bison shuffled his feet. 'Oh,' he snuffled. 'Sorry.' And he moved to one side.

Hare stood as straight and tall as possible and walked past. Angry Bison gazed at him, as if he was also struggling to make sense of it all.

Hare was getting braver by the second. His long ears danced jauntily. He strutted back and forth in front of Bison several times.

'There,' he said. 'You see? Easy, isn't it? You can move out of the way too.' Then, rather alarmed at the tone of his own voice he added: 'I'm going home now. Goodbye.' And with that Hare marched back to the little log cabin. His heart was beating fast.

It was only as he opened the front door that he suddenly remembered he was supposed to be warning Flamingo about the ghastly green soup. He stopped, looked back at a muddle-headed Bison staring after him and he sighed.

Anyhow, a rather unusual smell was drifting from the kitchen.

'Ah, where have you been?' asked Armadillo. He dipped a spoon into the saucepan and held it out to Hare. 'You're just in time to try this. I've added some cheese.'

Hare gulped. Was there no escape? The spoon was heading his way. He took a deep breath and closed his eyes. He took a tiny sip and sneezed violently.

Armadillo wiped his front. 'I didn't ask for it back,' he said.

'Peppery,' was all Hare could say. 'Sorry.' He went on to tell Armadillo about his meeting with Angry Bison.

'That was brave of you,' Armadillo declared, full of admiration.

'I don't think Bison is quite as angry as we thought,' said Hare.

'You are probably right, my long-eared friend. He was seeing everything as a problem. But then you helped him see that he was most of the problem himself. Well done, Hare!'

'I didn't know I was doing all that,' said Hare, tugging at one ear.

'Doesn't matter.' Armadillo shook his head and smiled. 'You did it. Now, let's take this Special Soup over to Flamingo.'

The two friends found a queue waiting patiently beside Flamingo's bath. Everyone wanted to help her recover from her

sore throat. Tortoise had brought a small bunch of flowers. Elephant presented her with a mudpack.

Bear (of the polar variety) had brought first aid.

'I'm almost a doctor,' he growled. 'Bandages are always a good idea.'

Giraffe handed her a small teddy. 'I've had it since I was born. It's always been a comfort for me. Please don't suck it.'

Flamingo raised her enormous beak and sniffed at Armadillo's Special Soup. 'Oh, Pops darling, you shouldn't have!'

But it was Lobster who brought the cure – a small jar of sea water. 'Salt water is a well-known cure for a sore throat. Have you ever seen a lobster with a sore throat? Or a

fish? No, because we gargle sea water all day.'

Flamingo was ecstatic. 'Sea water! Oh – so calming, so healing. Lobster, sweetie! You have extinguished the raging bonfires in my blazing gullet. Thank you!'

Lobster puffed out her chest and gave everyone a triumphant look. 'Once I knew Flamingo had a sore throat, it was obvious she would need my help.'

Giraffe rolled his eyes. Elephant murmured, 'Phoowee' very quietly, and wondered if he could have his mudpack back.

Jaguar turned to Armadillo and purred in his ear, 'Do you think lobsters taste nice? I was just wondering.' She might have winked as she spoke. Hare wasn't sure.

Animal or Vegetable?

All night long Flamingo had serenaded the full moon as it floated through the starry heavens. Armadillo snored and dreamed of giant cheese sandwiches. Outside, beneath the creamy moon, Armadillo's vegetables grew. And grew.

Morning arrived. Armadillo opened his eyes, only to see a long bean hanging over his open window sill. His eyes widened. The big leaves around it made it look like Elephant's head and trunk.

'Hare! Come and look at this!'

Hare came into Armadillo's bedroom,

stifling a yawn that quickly turned into a chuckle. 'It is Elephant, isn't it?' Hare went to the window and looked out. 'Have you seen your vegetables this morning? Come and look.'

They stared out of the window. Cucumbers and beans were climbing up the side of the house and had reached the roof. It looked as if the sky had been raining tomatoes all night.

Hare scratched his ears. 'I know the full moon helps plants grow but this is extraordinary.'

'It's a vegetable explosion,' Armadillo grunted. 'What am I going to do with them all?'

The pair studied the invading plants.

'That bean really does look like Elephant,' Hare remarked.

But Armadillo was having a struggle. When a cardigan has three sleeves instead of two, it's hard to know which sleeve to choose when you've only just got up.

'Actually, Hare, that bean looking like Elephant has given me an idea. We could have a vegetable competition. Why don't we ask everyone to use our extra vegetables to make models of themselves, or each other, or just things? That might get rid of the whole lot!'

'Bear made from tomatoes and beans!' shouted Hare.

'Angry Cucumber Bison!' added Armadillo, before they both fell to the floor, heaving with laughter.

Word went out about the competition and it was astonishing how quickly the pile of vegetables went down. Wombat filled the front basket on her bicycle twenty-six times. Elephant took half the tomatoes.

Even Tortoise made seven slow trips. 'But I have eaten some,' he confessed. 'Is that allowed?'

'Eat as much as you like.' Armadillo smiled as he watched the pile go down.

Jaguar spent a long time selecting a cucumber, a few beans and a small, unripe tomato.

'Is that all?' asked Armadillo, disappointed.

'Dignity is everything,' Jaguar answered over her shoulder as she padded gracefully away.

Only Flamingo took nothing. That was because Armadillo and Hare had asked her to be one of the judges, along with themselves.

'Darlings!' she cried. 'I am dazzled beyond dazzlement. Of course I shall be a judge. And afterwards, we shall dance and sing! We shall prance in all our bling! And I shall wear – oh, you will be amazed!' Flamingo's eyes shone like entire galaxies. 'Darlings, I am fabulous in pink! I can't wait!'

Flamingo was not the only excited creature in the Big Forest. The animals hid themselves away as they worked on their vegetable creations.

Competition Day arrived, and in the early evening the animals began to gather at

Flamingo's bath beside the lake.

Flamingo filled lanterns with fireflies.
Giraffe brought his chandelier and hung it
on a high branch. Bear set up his drum kit.

Hare settled with his tuba and Invisible Stick Insect struck up on the triangle. Ping! The music began. As Hare blew into his magical instrument, out floated balloons, party hats, rainbow bubbles and vegetables of every variety.

One by one the animals paraded their creations.

Elephant had smothered himself in tomatoes. 'I'm the Ketchup Elephant,' he said. 'Phoowee! Sorry about all the flies.'

Armadillo found himself thinking about dignity, but then he saw Tortoise.

Tortoise had carefully placed a layer of overlapping cucumbers down his back. They looked like scales. Thin beans stuck out of his mouth like whiskers.

Hare clapped his paws. 'That's you, Armadillo! Isn't Tortoise clever? He's even got your red slippers with the curled-up toes.'

'Oh yes,' murmured Armadillo. 'Red peppers on the feet. Ingenious.'

Giraffe strode majestically past the judges. He was covered from head to toe with all the bean poles which still had beans clinging to them. 'I am Invisible Beanstick Insect,' he announced.

Lobster jumped up. 'Disqualified! We can see you. You're not invisible at all!'

'Oh, Lobster, give it a rest!' snapped Armadillo. 'We're just having fun.'

In reply, Lobster stretched out her claws.

Bits of spinach and coriander hung down like wings. A necklace of radishes was draped round her neck, and on her head was a crown of broccoli.

'Darling!' cried Flamingo. 'How sweet. It's a tiny green me! Look, everyone. A green flamingo!'

Jaguar entered the arena. She held up her work. A single, long cucumber had thin beans sticking out on either side like legs. At one end of the cucumber there was a small, green tomato head.

'Invisible Stick Insect and I made this together,' Jaguar explained. 'It is a portrait of her. Normally she's so like a twig you can't see her, but now you can.'

Wombat had wrapped herself in cabbage

and lettuce leaves. Being a rather round animal she was able to roll along the ground past the judges' feet. 'I'm a pea!' she called out as she bundled 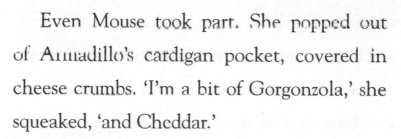 past them and crashed into a bush.

Even Mouse took part. She popped out of Armadillo's cardigan pocket, covered in cheese crumbs. 'I'm a bit of Gorgonzola,' she squeaked, 'and Cheddar.'

Finally, Bear appeared. He casually tossed a long colourful scarf round his neck. It had been made from green leaves, red peppers and courgette flowers. Bear posed himself carefully. From behind his back he produced the longest cucumber the Big Forest had ever seen. It had been carefully sliced in half lengthways. Bear raised the two halves to the top of his head and held them there, pointing at the sky.

'It's you, Hare!' yelled Armadillo, leaping to his feet. 'With cucumber ears! Bravo!' Everyone was laughing. The judges huddled together and a decision was made. Flamingo raised her wings and stepped forward.

'Darlings! What a wonderful extravaganza! But we must have a winner. Who will it be! Yes, the judges have agreed. Bear (of the whatsit variety) – you are our champion. Well done! And now, music! Dancing! Thrills and frills, mostly pink ones.'

The band was about to start when a dark, hulking figure stepped out of the Big Forest. It was Angry Bison. A tense silence descended. But Bison looked different. He was a meek and mild bison.

'I've come to apologise to you all for my rudeness,' Bison began. 'And before I go, I wanted to thank Hare for making me realise how it feels. I must hurry now. I have to tell all the others. I really must dash. It's such good news.'

Bison turned and made a last crashing disappearance amongst the trees.

'Thank me for what?' asked Hare, mystified. 'What others?'

Armadillo smiled into the darkness. 'There's more than one angry bison in the world. They usually arrive in giant herds, all thundering along at the same time. They don't give way to anything. You made him understand how uncomfortable that is for anyone in the way. And now he's gone! Strike up the band!'

Soon the band was blasting away. Flamingo disappeared into her wardrobe and closed the door. Most of the animals began to dance.

Armadillo collapsed onto a bench and watched. Hare knew that Armadillo hated dancing, so he joined his companion.

'What an evening,' Hare remarked. 'I did think Bear was brilliant.'

'Oh, he had you perfectly,' chuckled Armadillo, 'especially when he just stood there, posing.'

'I don't do that, do I?' asked Hare, rather shocked at the idea.

'Not deliberately. But when you stand still you do sometimes look as if you're practising to become a statue.'

'Oh dear. Oh dear.'

'Not at all, my dear chap. We all love you for it. Now get back in there and carry on blowing into your tuba. I shall strike a pose of my own on this bench.'

But Hare was hardly on his feet when a loud 'Oooooh!' went up from the crowd. The wardrobe doors swung open and out stepped Flamingo. She was a shimmering coral vision.

Bear was drumming up an earthquake. Invisible Stick Insect even managed to dent her triangle.

Flamingo opened her beak and sang. Her voice soared and swooped. The more she sang the higher she went, barely flapping her wings in a glorious aerial dance. She seemed to glow with stardust as she twisted and turned, folding and opening her wings like great fans.

Finally, Flamingo floated slowly back to earth, and as her toes touched the ground she slowly slid into the splits.

The crowd went wild.

Armadillo wiped a small tear from the corner of one eye. 'Genius,' he whispered. 'Sheer genius.'

'Phoowee,' murmured Elephant, crossing his legs. 'That must hurt a bit.'

Late that night, Armadillo and Hare made their way home across the moonlit meadow.

'I do think Flamingo is quite the most extraordinary creature,' Armadillo murmured.

'Yes,' Hare answered slowly. He was lost in his own thoughts. 'You know, I hardly said anything to Bison. I don't see how I could have changed him.'

Armadillo threw an arm round Hare's shoulders as they walked. 'Sometimes a few simple words achieve much more than grand speeches,' he said. 'Come on. Let's get home. It's late and the cheese is calling me.'

Thousands of miles above them, the stars silently glittered in the deep, dark sky. Flamingo's lilting voice drifted over the treetops as she sang a last lullaby for all the friends in the Big Forest.

Armadillo and Hare's Short Discussion

Armadillo and Hare were sitting out on the porch and watching the sun set behind the Big Forest. Armadillo stretched out his legs and settled his toes comfortably in his slippers.

'You know,' began Hare, 'you said that one day you would tell me the story of your favourite slippers.'

'Hmm. Are you sure you're not just putting off doing the washing-up? You do know it's your turn?'

'Of course, but I told you all about my tuba, and now I want to know about your slippers.'

'Very well,' said Armadillo. 'It was several years before you arrived here and one afternoon there was a knock at the door. When I opened it I saw a creature I had never seen the like of. She had beautiful reddy-brown fur and a very bushy tail with stripes. She told me she was a red panda and had come from Nepal.'

'Nepal?' Hare was astonished. 'She had travelled all that way to the Big Forest?'

'Quite,' nodded Armadillo. 'She said she was journeying around the world and she needed somewhere safe to stay for a night or two. Of course I couldn't say "no". In the end she stayed for a week.

'She told me some wonderful tales about the places she had been. Then one evening I noticed that she had beautiful blue soft-leather shoes. She said they were the most comfortable shoes she had ever had. I held them and couldn't believe how soft the leather was.

'Eventually she went travelling on, and I never saw her again. But a year and three days later a small parcel arrived. When I opened it there were these red slippers that I am wearing now. There was a note, thanking me for the time we spent together. She had finally travelled back to her own country and family.'

Armadillo stopped for a moment. 'I guess you could say that my slippers have almost as much story in them as your tuba.'

Hare nodded happily. 'It's nice to have something like that to remember someone by.'

Armadillo nodded. 'Small things are the most important things of all,' he said. He nodded wisely and looked across at Hare. 'And I think there are several important small things in the sink that need washing up.'

Hare pulled a face and sighed. 'All right. I'm going.'